INSTRUCTIONS

Build your own LEGO® NEXO KNIGHTS™ hero.

FLASH OF EVIL

Monstrox is back and he's more evil than ever! With one zap of his lightning, he turns Jestro into a villain again. Number the pictures to put them in the right order and find out what happened.

Can you spot Monstrox in the first picture of the sequence?

FORBIDDEN POWERS

To destroy Knighton, Jestro and his evil minions need to find the Forbidden Powers that Merlok hid around the realm. Find the matching pairs of symbols. The symbol without a matching pair will reveal the coordinates of the next area they plan to attack. Circle their destination on page 5.

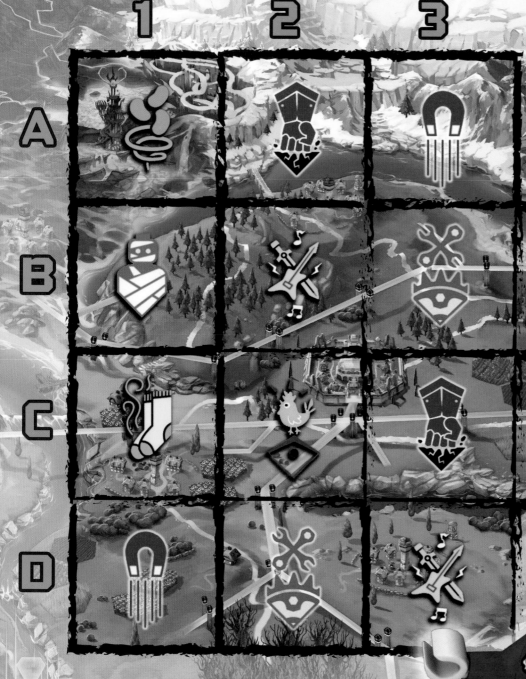

A4 Snottingham

A1 Lava Lands

D3 Waterton

C1 Bookingham

Use a black pencil to fill in all the number '1' shapes and a purple pencil on the number '2' shapes to reveal Clay's opponent. Remember to leave all the number '3' shapes white.

ALL TOGETHER NOW!

Help Lance defeat the evil Cloud of Monstrox and his Stone Monster army by sending in the other NEXO KNIGHTS heroes. Mark which route each Knight should take through the maze to reach Lance. Remember they can only move across the symbols of their own shields!

LANCE

POWER MATCH!

Jestro managed to get his hands on another Forbidden Power called Relentless Rust, and he is ready to use it! Which power is it? Look at Jestro's tablet and find its exact copy.

A

B

C

D

E

F

G

PERFECT SHOT

PICTURE GLITCH

Lance is editing photos of himself on Ava's computer. But he's not exactly an expert at it! Fix his cut-up photo on the opposite page by numbering the pieces to put them in the right order. Use the picture on this page to help you work out where each piece goes.

INCOMPLETE INVENTIONS

Robin built these cool new Battle Suits in a big hurry and now each one is missing something! Can you help him put the parts in the right places?

THE POWER OF UNITY

Stone Monsters can only be defeated by using extra special Combo Powers! Look at the first power chosen by Merlok 2.0 and find two more that will help him achieve the power score of 100 per cent!

POWER LEVEL

33% | 100%

SCAN THE POWER

? ?

20%

28%

5%

68%

36%

47%

THE TROUBLE WITH TOMATOES

With one flick of his sword, Clay dispatched two Bouldrons.

'That's the last trouble you'll cause in Tomatoton!' said Clay, striking a victory pose. 'All right, NEXO KNIGHTS team – let's do a last sweep through town to make sure we got them all.'

Axl started searching Tomatoton for evildoers. He turned a corner and nearly knocked over a large cooking pot that was sitting on top of a big fire. He was about to continue on his way when his nostrils caught a whiff of something tasty.

'That smells delicious!' Axl told the peasant tending the pot. 'What is it?'

'I'm making salsa,' said the peasant. 'Our tomatoes are the biggest and most delicious in the land. But my recipe is missing something. I would love some help from a celebrity chef such as yourself to make it better.'

Axl knew he needed to make sure all the enemies were gone . . . but the salsa needed him too. Axl let his stomach decide. 'I can help you,' he answered. 'Do you have any coriander?'

Later, the Fortrex rumbled over cobblestone roads on the way home. Axl had kicked his feet up and was enjoying the fresh salsa he had helped prepare. The Fortrex could be a bumpy ride at times and Axl was wearing as much salsa as he was managing to get into his mouth!

The Knights felt the Fortrex suddenly brake and swing 180 degrees. Aaron, seated next to Axl, was now wearing salsa too.

'Really?' cried Aaron. 'To be fair though, I do enjoy wearing delicious salsa as much as eating it.'

'Sorry,' said Axl. He took a tortilla chip, slid it along Aaron's breastplate to clean off most of the salsa, and then ate it. 'All better,' said Axl. 'Delicious!'

Clay walked in. 'We must have missed some monsters. Let's go!'

When the Fortrex pulled back into Tomatoton, the heroes jumped into action again.

'Spread out, team!' said Clay. 'Aaron, I need eyes from above.'

Aaron rode his hover shield high into the air. 'Are you guys lost?' he joked, surprising a few Bouldrons with a couple of shots from his crossbow.

One of the Bouldrons dived from the tower to escape. SPLUUUSH! It landed in the big pot of salsa.

'NOOOOO! MY SALSA!' screamed Axl.

'*Your* salsa?' Lance gave Axl a puzzled look. The monster attempted to escape but, having just leaped out of the salsa, he left a tasty and very visible trail, so Lance gave chase.

Macy spun around and swung at the Bouldron that was unfortunate enough to cross her path.

'Hey, Axl,' said Macy, 'weren't you meant to check this area was clear after the battle?'

Axl answered nervously. 'Yes, I was here. I did check, but I didn't see any monsters! Really!' Axl knew that this was ALL his fault.

A while later, the Fortrex rumbled through Tomatoton towards home for the second time that day. Axl felt bad and called everyone together to apologize. He told them how he had been distracted by … salsa.

The other Knights were a bit disappointed in Axl, but they appreciated him telling them the truth.

'I completely understand,' said Lance. 'You know, when I'm supposed to be doing something important and someone wants to take pictures of me, it's very hard to say "no".' Lance paused, then added, 'I'll go back later and let them admire my amazing good looks.'

'Tomatoton grows tasty tomatoes,' said Clay. 'Let's have a taste of that salsa you made.'

'Well, that's the thing,' said Axl sheepishly. 'I ate all the salsa so … I don't suppose we could swing by Chipshire?'

SHIELD SNATCHER

The **NEXO KNIGHTS** heroes are in trouble – Robot Hoodlum stole their shields. He's only supposed to steal from the rich! Help the team find their five shields hidden in Rock Wood Forest.

> HA! IT'S NOT JUST THE SHIELDS THAT ARE HIDDEN AROUND HERE! CAN YOU SPOT SIX OF MY MERRY MECH COMRADES?

WHAT DOES HE NEED OUR SHIELDS FOR?

I DON'T KNOW ABOUT YOURS, BUT I BET HE STOLE MINE SO HE COULD GET IT AUTOGRAPHED!

QUEEN IN DISTRESS

Jestro has kidnapped Queen Halbert! Help Clay by untangling the lines to find out which of the three vehicles is carrying the queen. Quick! There's no time to lose!

START

MACY'S DOUBLE

LIVING STATUES

The Museum Gala has attracted the kingdom's most important celebrities, including the king and his mech. Macy is even wearing a dress! Look at the statues and find the odd figure out in each of the three groups.

THE ROLLING BROTHERS

The Cloud of Monstrox and Jestro need very powerful allies to battle the NEXO KNIGHTS heroes. They are looking for help from the legendary Granite Golems – the Rolling Brothers. Find Reex, Roog and Rumble by matching the faces on Roberto Arnoldi's scroll below to the faces in the rocks.

I DON'T GET IT. WHO NEEDS STONE MONSTERS WHEN THERE'S A WHOLE ARMY OF MY CREATIONS?

A

B

C

WAIT, WEREN'T THERE THREE OF US?

YEAH, BUT THE THIRD ONE OF US DOESN'T LOOK MUCH LIKE YOU OR ME.

DRAW A MONSTER

You think that the Cloud of Monstrox is the only one who can create monsters? Nonsense! It's time for you to design your own Stone Monster! All you have to do is draw it.

IF YOUR MONSTER IS AS TERRIFYING AS MY CREATIONS, MAYBE I'LL GIVE YOU A JOB!

What are you going to call your monster? Remember, a cool name makes all the difference.

My monster's name is ....